This Little Tiger book belongs to:

_____

_____

_____

_____

For Nadia and Paul
~ A H B

LITTLE TIGER PRESS
An imprint of Magi Publications
1 The Coda Centre, 189 Munster Road,
London SW6 6AW
www.littletigerpress.com

First published in Great Britain 2004
This edition published 2005

Text copyright © A H Benjamin 2004
Illustrations copyright © John Bendall-Brunello 2004
A H Benjamin and John Bendall-Brunello have
asserted their rights to be identified as the author
and illustrator of this work under the Copyright,
Designs and Patents Act, 1988
Printed in Dubai by Oriental Press

ISBN 1 84506 003 2

A CIP catalogue record for this book
is available from the British Library

2 4 6 8 10 9 7 5 3 1

At the End of the
Rainbow

A H Benjamin & John Bendall-Brunello

LITTLE TIGER PRESS

London

"Wow!" gasped Badger and Fox.
"It's beautiful!"
A bright, clear rainbow
hung in the sky
like a jewel.

Badger and Fox stood gazing at the bright colours.

Then Badger said, "You know, there's treasure at the end of a rainbow!"

"What's treasure?" asked Fox.

"I'm not sure," replied Badger, "but I think it's gold or silver or jewels – something that will make you rich for ever and ever!"

"Let's go and find this treasure!" cried Fox excitedly.

And they were off, racing towards the nearby woods.

As the two friends hurried along
all they could think of was treasure.
   What did it look like? Was it big
or small? What colour was it?
Just then they noticed Squirrel,
sitting in front of a pile of acorns.

"My treasure,"
he was singing
to himself. "My
beautiful treasure!"

Badger and Fox scampered up to Squirrel.

"Go away!" he ordered. "You're not stealing my treasure!"

"That's not treasure," said Fox, "that's just a pile of acorns."

"It's treasure to me," replied Squirrel. "It's my food for the winter. What's more important than that?"

"Well we're going to find the real thing!" said Badger, and the friends raced off.

Soon Badger and Fox came to
a small river. Among the reeds they
spotted Mother Duck.

"My little treasure!" she was calling.
"Where are you?"

Badger and Fox were curious.

"Are you looking for treasure?" they asked.

"Yes, my own little treasure," replied
Mother Duck. "Oh look, there he is!"

A golden, fluffy
duckling came pattering along.
Mother Duck tucked him under her wing.
"Don't disappear like that," she said gently.
"You'll have me worried, my treasure."
Badger and Fox looked puzzled.
"Is that your treasure?" they said.
"Of course," smiled Mother Duck proudly.
"I love my baby more than anything in the
world, so he is a treasure to me. Aren't you,
my little one? Now let's go home."

Badger and Fox rushed on, eager to find their treasure at the end of the rainbow. They clambered up a steep, bumpy hill, and found Old Hare sitting at the top.

"Hello, there!" he greeted.

"Hello!" called the friends. "We're
on our way to find treasure!"

"Ahh," nodded Old Hare. "I have
lots of that."

"Really? Where?" they asked.

Old Hare patted his head. "Here," he said. "My memories are my treasure. They make me happy."

"What are memories?" asked Badger.

"They're all that you remember from the past," said Old Hare. "Things you've done, places you've visited, friends you've loved. Your adventure today will become a memory you'll treasure, one day. So enjoy yourselves, little ones!"

"Goodbye!" called Badger and Fox. And they were off, sliding down the other side of the hill.

Just then thick, dark clouds filled the sky.
The rainbow vanished. It started to rain,
harder and harder. Badger and Fox had
to take shelter.

"We'll never find our treasure now,"
said Badger miserably.

As they waited
for the rain to
stop, the friends
remembered
Squirrel. How
happy he was just
to have enough food.
And Mother Duck and
her love for her baby.

Old Hare was happy too, because he had his memories. They all had their own kind of treasure ... Maybe treasure wasn't gold and silver and jewels. It was what you loved, something very special, and something that made you happy.

Fox looked at Badger and Badger looked at Fox ...

"You're a treasure!" said Badger,
jumping up.

"You're a treasure too," said Fox,
skipping around.

And they started laughing and
dancing until they could dance
no more!

At last the rain stopped and the sun came out again. The two friends happily made their way back home. Far, far behind them a new rainbow had appeared in the sky. But neither Badger nor Fox noticed.

More treasures from Little Tiger Press

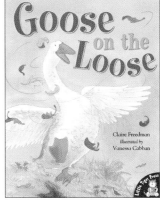